For my children.
—Hena

For my wonderful Mama, Baba, and Dada
and with thanks for immense support from Ian M, Ian W, and Tom.
—Saffa

A note from the author:

The phrase "inshallah" is something I say throughout my day when making any plan or wishing anything for the future—from the most basic everyday intentions to my biggest dreams. It means "if God wills it" in Arabic and is something that Muslims around the globe hear from the moment they are born and are taught to express as they learn to speak. The phrase, however, goes beyond Muslims in popular culture, and today is used throughout the Arabic speaking world by people of many faiths to reflect the idea of a greater force or power beyond ourselves. It's a common theme found in other languages and cultures as well, such as "ojalá" in Spanish or "God willing" in English.

As a parent, my most frequent prayers and wishes are for my children, and the phrase inshallah is intertwined with each and every one. In uncertain times, it offers me comfort and strength. This book celebrates both the phrase and a mother's love and hopes for her child. Every line, or wish, in the book is inspired by the Quran, the Muslim holy book, which offers guidelines on how to live a thoughtful and grounded life filled with fairness, charity, justice, and most of all, love. These are universal values that transcend any particular belief system, and I hope they will resonate with all readers.

Text copyright © 2020 by Hena Khan.
Illustrations copyright © 2020 by Saffa Khan.

Library of Congress Cataloging-in-Publication Data available.

ISBN 978-1-4521-8019-9

Manufactured in China.

MIX
Paper from
responsible sources
FSC™ C008047

Design by Abbie Goveia.
Art direction by Amelia Mack.
Typeset in Orange Juice.
The illustrations in this book were primarily rendered digitally,
with ink for strokes and texture.

10 9 8 7 6 5 4 3 2

Chronicle Books LLC
680 Second Street
San Francisco, California 94107

Chronicle Books—we see things differently.
Become part of our community at www.chroniclekids.com.

LIKE the MOON LOVES the SKY

By **HENA KHAN**

Illustrated by **SAFFA KHAN**

chronicle books · san francisco

Inshallah you are all
that is gentle and good.

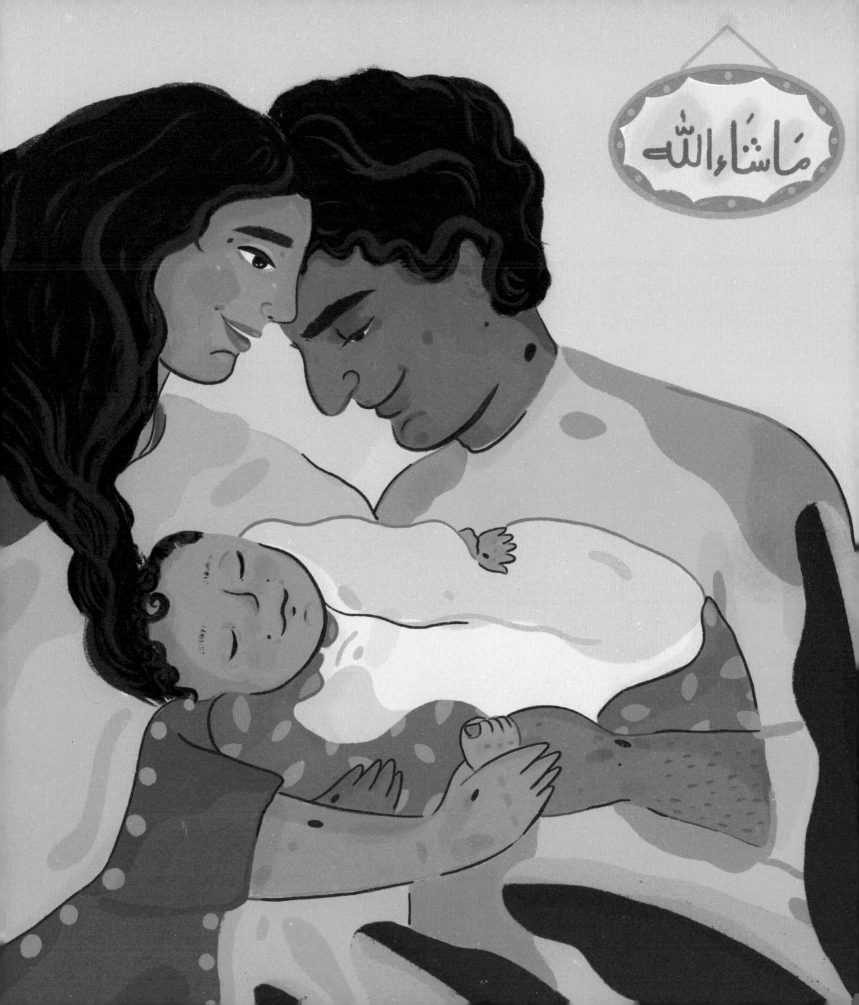

Inshallah you feel safe,
like all children should.

Inshallah you are kind
to those most in need.

Inshallah you stand strong,
like a tree with firm roots.

Inshallah you plant gardens
filled with sweet fruits.

Inshallah you have faith
that won't waver or bend.

Inshallah you are thoughtful
of plans that you make.

Inshallah you speak truth
and work for its sake.

Inshallah you travel
to thrilling new places.

Inshallah you find wonder
in birds as they fly.

Inshallah you are loved,
like the moon loves the sky.